# PARTY GIRLS POPSTARS

## Michelle: Centre Stage

# PARTY GIRLS POPSTARS

## Michelle: Centre Stage

### Jennie Walters

illustrated by Jessie Eckel

**Hodder Children's Books**

a division of Hodder Headline Limited

# For Olivia and Abigail

Special thanks to David Grindrod and Sam Dixon-Szul
for their helpful advice

First published in Great Britain in 2002
by Hodder Children's Books

A Catalogue record for this book
is available from the British Library

ISBN 0 340 85411 1

Typeset by Hewer Text Ltd, Edinburgh
Printed and bound in Great Britain by
Bookmarque Ltd, Croydon, Surrey

Hodder Children's Books
a division of Hodder Headline Ltd
338 Euston Road
London NW1 3BH

# FAME FACT FILE: MICHELLE

**Fave dance wear:** crop tops, sloppy T-shirts, bandannas, stretch trousers or leggings, dance shoes

**Lucky charm:** silver ring my gran gave me

**Stage superstition:** not wearing anything yellow or green on stage

**First role:** Mary, in my nursery school nativity play

**Worst stage moment:** falling off the edge in rehearsals for 'Grease' and spraining my ankle

**Best stage moment:** a standing ovation at the end of the show

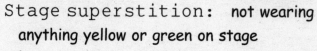

**Best tip for nerves:** keep breathing and keep smiling! Pretend everyone loves you

**Ambition:** to become a star, of course!

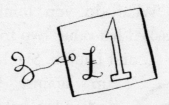

'How about this, Miche?' Caz called, pulling an orange satin shirt with a wide floppy collar off the rack and holding it up for her friend to see.

'Maybe.' Michelle gave the shirt a quick first inspection. Stretching over a woman who was bent double rifling through the skirts, she grabbed it from Caz's hands for a closer look and then made her way to the mirror in another corner of the charity shop.

You had to be quick if you spotted a bargain in this place. Michelle had been about to try on a pair of groovy platform shoes when an old lady with wispy grey hair had snatched them up and carried them off before she could open her mouth. Well, they'd look just great with her baggy tracksuit trousers, wouldn't they? The perfect finishing touch. Jess had happened to see what was going on and, when she caught Michelle's eye, they'd both collapsed in a fit of giggles.

'What do you think?' Michelle asked her other two friends, Sunny and Lauren. She held the shirt up against herself and studied her reflection, trying to decide whether the colour suited her olive skin and brown hair. 'It's a bit big, isn't it?'

'That doesn't matter. You could easily take it in,' Lauren said, stretching out one of the sleeves to examine it properly. She was always finding second-hand clothes which, with a few subtle alterations, ended up looking funky and fantastic. Today, she'd already snaffled a gorgeous denim skirt from one of the rails that Michelle had looked through and written off as a dead loss.

Sunny wrinkled her nose at Michelle's reflection. 'But have you seen that humungous great stain on the front?' she whispered, as though the shirt's previous owner might be lurking somewhere nearby.

'Oh, gross!' Michelle immediately jammed it back on a rail and wiped her hands fastidiously on her jeans. 'Come on, let's go. I don't think we're going to find anything here.'

OK, she'd told her drama teacher that she'd try and find some seventies gear for their mid-term summer show (a poptastic tribute to Abba) – but there were limits. Digging through heaps of old clothes in search of hidden treasure might be Lauren's idea of heaven, but Michelle was beginning to decide that it wasn't hers. It had taken some persuading from Lauren before she'd agreed to set foot in the charity shop to start off with. And she definitely didn't want to appear on stage with somebody else's dinner spilled down her front!

'Hey, look at this!' Jess was over by the scarves, waving something white and feathery in the air. 'Isn't it cool?'

Michelle made her way through to where Jess was standing and saw she had a fluffy feather boa in her hands. Now that looked a lot more promising! It was spotlessly clean, for one thing, and she could just picture one of the Abba girls wearing it. She wrapped it round her neck and flung one end over her shoulder, the downy feathers tickling her chin.

'Beautiful!' Jess said approvingly, and Caz agreed.

'This is great,' Michelle murmured, stroking the soft white plumage. 'Thanks, Jess!' She couldn't help imagining herself standing on stage under the glare of the spotlights, waiting for that magical moment when the music would begin and she could start singing. Without wanting to boast, she knew she had a good voice. But there was more to it than that: somehow she was able to grab the audience's attention and take them along with her until the very last note.

Ever since she was tiny, Michelle had loved performing. She used to sing for her mum and her gran all the time, and she was usually to be found in the dressing-up corner at nursery school. That's where she'd met Sunny, Jess and Lauren – plus Nikki, their other best mate who'd gone to live in California the year before. (Caz had moved into the area later on, next door to Lauren.) Ever since then, Michelle had been nagging her friends into putting on shows with her – naturally, she'd take the lead role – though once she'd started going to a proper class on Saturday mornings, where they studied dance and singing as well as drama, she'd eased off a little. Now she drove the others mad by constantly singing under her breath and practising her dance moves. They knew she couldn't really help it, though: she was stagestruck and that was that. It was in her blood.

She blew gently on the feathers to ruffle them, dreaming herself on stage in some big West End theatre. That was her secret ambition: to star in a professional show. One day, it might happen . . .

She craned to catch a glimpse of herself in the mirror, but a girl in a leather biker jacket was standing full square in front of it, browsing through a rack of records.

Still, Michelle didn't really need to see her gorgeous reflection to make up her mind. 'I'll take it,' she decided. The boa cost less than a pound, and it was the ideal Abba accessory. Her costume was under way!

'I don't know why you're looking round charity shops for your seventies outfit,' Jess's mum Trish said to Michelle later, when they were all sitting round in the café having something to eat. 'Why didn't you ask me? I've kept some of the trendy gear I used to wear back in the dark ages when I was a teenager. My Afghan coat might even be around somewhere – that belongs in a fashion museum.'

'A fashion disaster museum, you mean!' Jess snorted.

'Wow! Sounds amazing,' Michelle said politely, though privately she couldn't imagine Jess's mother ever having been trendy, even when she was young. She'd lived a few doors down the road from Jess most of her life, so she knew all the Fitzgerald family really well. Trish was nice, but no one could ever accuse her of being over-interested in fashion. And while she wasn't exactly fat, she was – well, motherly would be a good way of putting it. Her clothes would be bound to swamp Michelle.

Somehow Trish seemed to know what she was thinking. 'I was a size eight when I was a teenager,' she said. 'And my waist was so tiny, Andy could put both hands around it and still have room to spare.'

'Mum! Too much information!' Jess squealed in embarrassment. 'Do we really need to know the weird things you and Dad got up to when you were young?'

'Maybe not,' her mother smiled. 'But I'll bring some bags down from the loft this afternoon and you girls can have a look through. I bet you'll be surprised.'

Michelle had to admit she *was* surprised by the contents of the suitcase Trish eventually managed to find up in the loft at the Fitzgeralds' house. There were some great clothes there – clothes that it was hard to imagine Jess's plump and comfortable mother ever wearing. She brought the case down to the sitting room where Jess and Michelle were listening to music (Caz, Lauren and Sunny having been dropped off at home), along with a big cardboard box.

'Now this is going to be a trip down Memory Lane,' she said, wrestling with the rusty catches on the case. Eventually she got them open and raised the lid, releasing a musty smell of mothballs and old clothes. But everything was clean, and neatly packed away in tissue paper. First came the tops: a stripy cheesecloth shirt, a blue tie-dye T-shirt with long flared sleeves, and a sleeveless vest-type thing Trish called a tank top (Michelle wouldn't be seen dead in *that*!). Then she took out a pink and orange crochet mini-dress, followed by a long blue one with tiny buttons all the way up the front and a droopy collar.

'My first Biba dress,' she sighed, stroking the crinkly material. 'I was so proud of it! My friend Diane and I went down to London to buy them together. Hers was just the same, only pink. We thought we were the bees' knees at the disco in those, I can tell you.'

'Oh, wow! This is fantastic!' Michelle exclaimed, pouncing on a white miniskirt printed all over with shiny circles. She held it up against herself to see if it would fit and decided there was every chance: being tall sometimes had its advantages. Michelle often felt self-conscious about her height, though their dance teacher told her to be proud of it. She had to stand up straight and throw those shoulders back!

'I remember wearing that to a David Cassidy concert,' Trish said fondly, sitting back on her heels. 'With . . . wait a minute, I know they're here somewhere.' She'd started to rummage in the box. 'Yes! Feast your eyes on these.' And she drew out a pair of white platform boots.

'Oh, Mum! Those are amazing!' Jess said, already unzipping one of the boots to try it on. 'What size are they?'

'Four, I think,' her mother replied. 'I always had dainty feet.'

Michelle kicked off her trainers and put on the other boot. Just like Cinderella's glass slipper, it fitted her perfectly!

'Oh, please, Trish! Please can I borrow these boots for the show? And the miniskirt too?' she begged, balancing precariously on one high platform sole. She would look so good in the mini and boots, with maybe a halterneck top of her own – and the feather boa, of course. It was the perfect outfit!

\* \* \*

'You can't really be thinking of wearing those boots! We'll look ridiculous together!'

It was Tiffany Wells speaking, Michelle's least favourite person in the drama class. They were standing side by side in front of a full-length mirror, backstage in the school hall where the 'Thank You For The Music: Abba Spectacular' show was going to take place. The curtain would be rising in about half an hour.

'I don't even come up to your shoulder,' Tiffany went on, gazing at the two of them in the mirror. 'Everyone'll burst out laughing as soon as they see us.'

Michelle glowered at Tiffany's reflection. She hated to admit it, but she did look like a giant in those platform boots – especially next to Tiffany. It was such a pity though! The boots made her legs seem really long and slim, and they suited the miniskirt perfectly. Why did Tiffany have to be so short? If she was normal-sized, they wouldn't have such a problem. This was all her fault!

Tiffany usually managed to make Michelle feel clumsy and awkward. She was a petite little thing, with wavy blonde hair that always looked perfect, a snub nose dusted with freckles and vivid blue eyes. The only thing about her that wasn't small was her voice: she could really belt the numbers out. And her big head, Michelle added to herself. Tiffany thought she was the best thing to have ever come out of the Spotlight Saturday drama group. She behaved like everyone else was an amateur and she was a professional – just because she went to extra dance classes and sang in the choir at whichever posh school it was that she went to.

But though Tiffany might be irritating, she did have a point. Reluctantly, Michelle decided the boots would have to go, no matter how great they looked. 'I've got some stripy socks that'll do instead,' she sighed, starting to unzip the boots. 'They stretch over my knees, which is quite seventies, isn't it? And I can wear them with my dance shoes.'

'Much better,' Tiffany said, finally tearing herself away from the mirror. 'At least we won't look like Little and Large.'

Michelle stuck out her tongue quickly while

Tiffany's back was turned. OK, it was childish, but it made her feel better. Of course the next second she was worried that Tiffany had spotted her out of the corner of one eye. 'I like your minidress,' she said, trying to be nice. 'Where did you get it from?'

'My mother hired it from this fantastic place she found on the Internet,' Tiffany replied, smoothing the swirly psychedelic fabric with such a smug look that Michelle wanted to take her perfect blonde hair and give it a good hard tug.

Once she'd changed out of the boots, there wasn't really anything else left for Michelle to do. Her hair and make-up were done, so she was ready to go. To take her mind off things, she wandered through the backstage area towards the stage. She could hear Mr Scott playing a medley of Abba songs on the piano as the hall began to fill up with people. A hum of conversation seeped through the thick stage curtain, punctuated by the occasional scrape and clatter of chair legs. She put her eye to the narrow gap between the curtain and the wall, and took a peek at the audience. Some of the parents were wearing seventies clothes: there were fathers in kipper ties and corduroy suits, and mothers in cheesecloth. Mega embarrassing! Michelle was glad her own mum was too young to have anything like that tucked away at the back of her wardrobe.

And then she spotted Jess, Caz, Lauren and Sunny, sitting together with her mum, Jess's and Lauren's in the row behind them. Great! Knowing they were there, rooting for her, gave Michelle a warm glow. A tingle of anticipation began to grow in place of her nerves, and she found herself smiling. She'd make her friends proud!

Forty-five minutes later, the show was over –
and Michelle was wishing they could do it all
again. 'Can't we sing another encore?' she
begged their dance teacher as the curtain fell
for the last time, her face flushed with excitement
and her eyes sparkling. 'Please? Listen – they're
still clapping out there!'

'I know, but two encores are definitely
enough,' she replied, laughing. 'Well done!
You were all fantastic. I was so proud of you!'

'Oh, it was the best!' Michelle said, looking
around for other people in the cast to celebrate
with. Everyone seemed to be on a high: leaping
around like maniacs and hugging each other.
The Abba spectacular had been a huge success!
Everybody in the hall was on their feet for the

curtain call; they'd all danced along to the reprise of 'Waterloo', the first encore, and 'Thank you for the Music', the second. Michelle hadn't wanted it ever to end.

'You were great, Tiffany,' she said, feeling so happy she could afford to be generous.

'So were you,' Tiffany replied, beaming. 'I think our voices go really well together, don't you?'

Maybe Tiffany's not so bad after all, Michelle thought to herself as the two of them went off to change out of their stage clothes and take off their make-up. But now she wanted to see her real friends: they were all going out for a pizza together and she couldn't wait to hear what they thought of the show.

'Hey there, you two!' It was Ella, the Spotlight singing teacher, hurrying up to Tiffany and Michelle with a tall, thin man in tow. 'I'm glad I've caught you together.' She put an arm round each of their shoulders and hugged them close. 'Well done! You sang beautifully tonight. And I want you to meet Richard, an old friend of mine from music college.'

'Now I know why Ella was so keen for me to come and hear you both,' Richard said, smiling. 'Congratulations! That was a great performance.'

'Thanks,' Michelle replied.

Tiffany added pertly, 'We enjoyed ourselves too,' before turning to go.

'And thanks for all your help, Ella,' Michelle said. She liked their singing teacher a lot: Ella was always bouncy and enthusiastic, and they'd learnt some great songs with her. She had a mass of brown hair in wild corkscrew curls that was forever falling into her eyes when she played the piano, and she always wore really interesting clothes – screen-printed T-shirts or vintage dresses with clumpy boots.

'Hang on a minute!' Ella said, grabbing Tiffany's arm to hold her back. 'We've got something important to tell you.' She waited until she had both girls' attention and then went on, 'Richard's an old friend of mine, but that's not all. He's a casting agent too. You know what that is, don't you?'

Michelle felt her stomach lurch with excitement. Her legs had suddenly turned to jelly. A casting agent sounded professional! 'You d-don't mean . . .?' she began, and then faltered to a halt. No point in jumping to the wrong conclusion and embarrassing herself. Besides, she hardly dared to put her hopes into words.

'Yes, I do,' Ella said, her eyes sparkling even more brightly than usual. 'Just listen to what he has to say. I think you'll find it quite interesting!'

And Michelle had to pinch herself to make sure she wasn't dreaming when Richard began to speak . . .

'He wants us to come to an audition in London, next Saturday. Me and Tiffany,' Michelle told the others, her eyes as wide as saucers. 'It's for a pop musical they're putting on next year – in the West End!' She could still hardly believe it herself.

They were sitting in the pizza house, waiting for their order to come. To begin with, all everyone had wanted talk about was the Abba show: how good the dancing was, how funky the cast had looked in their seventies gear, how great it had been to hear Michelle singing with a proper microphone. She'd let them witter on, hugging her fantastic secret close for a little while longer. At last she'd told her friends – and for a second, you could have heard a pin drop at their table. Then they all burst out talking at the same time.

'That's so amazing! What kind of musical is it?' 'Oh, wow! You're going to be famous!' 'You're so lucky! Can we come along too?' 'Will it be shown on TV?'

Eventually everybody calmed down enough for Michelle to fill them in on the details. The show was about three girls who grew up in the seventies and later formed a band together: how they struggled to succeed, and what happened to them when they hit the big time. Most of the action was going to centre around the adult actresses, but Richard was also looking for girls to play the stars in a couple of scenes when they were younger. He wanted to find a team of nine, so they could take it in turns to perform in groups of three and not have to work night after night without a break.

'At least that gives you more of a chance,' Sunny said, being practical. 'It's not like there's only one part up for grabs and you'd have to be a superstar to get it.'

'But she *is* a superstar!' Caz said, reaching up to pat Michelle on the head. 'And after tonight, how could he not give you a part?'

'It's not just Richard's decision, though,' Michelle told her, chewing on a plastic straw. 'There are going to be three auditions at least. The first one is just with Richard and the director's assistant. Then for the second one, we have to perform a song from the show in front of the choreographer and some other people as well. And then the last audition's on the actual stage, in front of the director!' It was a scary thought – but an exciting one too.

After Richard had broken the news about the audition to the girls, he'd had a word with both their mothers (Michelle could see her mum telling Jess's and Lauren's about it right now). Tiffany's mother had gone into overdrive, asking Richard a million questions about the show and acting as if it was obvious her daughter was going to be chosen. No one else could get a word in edgeways! She'd also told Tiffany very loudly that she'd book some more lessons with her voice coach at school – which Michelle thought was quite rude, with Ella standing there. She knew Mrs Wells didn't rate Ella because she was young and hadn't been teaching very long, but there was no need to make it so obvious. After all, if it hadn't been for Ella they probably wouldn't have heard about these auditions in the first place. And they certainly wouldn't have met Richard beforehand.

Just imagining the audition brought Michelle out in goosebumps. But surely Richard must have thought she was good enough or he'd never have asked her to enter, would he? Although she was trying so hard not to get carried away, a tiny voice inside her kept saying, 'This is your big chance – you'd better grab it with both hands! You know you can do it!' And she could see herself walking out on that West End stage already.

'I can't wait for half term,' Jess said, turning her face up to the sun with her eyes closed. 'D'you think the weather's going to stay fine next week?'

They were sitting squashed up together on a bench in the playground at school, waiting lazily for the dinner break to end. Five days had passed since the Abba show, and there were only one and a half more to go until the weekend and then the summer half-term holiday. A whole week off school! It couldn't come quickly enough. Sunny was going to stay with her cousins for a while but the others would be hanging out at home. There'd be plenty of time for sleepovers, shopping trips and spur-of-the-moment picnics.

'You're not going away are you, Shell?' Caz said, already dreaming up plans as she basked in the sunshine. 'Not going to stay with your gran or anything?'

'As if,' Michelle said, raising her eyebrows. She jumped up impatiently from the end of the bench and tugged down her skirt. 'Come on, Caz! I'm not going anywhere next week because—'

' – Because next week is audition week,' everyone else (except Caz) joined in.

'Have you been asleep or something?' Sunny added, prodding Caz in the ribs. 'It's not like Michelle hasn't told us twenty times a day.'

'Oh, yes. Of course.' Caz shut her eyes again. 'How could I have forgotten?'

Michelle twirled around, humming under her breath, and started waving one arm as though she had a fly trapped up her sleeve.

'What are you doing?' Lauren asked, staring at her.

'Practising my arm movements. What does it look like?' Michelle replied tersely.

'Well, sor-ree! There's no need to bite my head off.' Lauren was obviously offended.

Michelle stopped twirling and waving. 'Sorry. I'm a bit nervous, that's all,' she said, sitting back down on the bench again. 'D'you really think I've chosen the right song? What if lots of other people go for that one too? And I'm not sure whether to dance along or not. Look – I made up this routine last night.' She jumped up again, as edgy as a cat on hot bricks, while the others tried to look interested.

'I think it's definitely the best song,' Sunny yawned. 'We've been though this already, haven't we?'

Michelle was going to perform part of a number that a girl group called Candy had brought out a couple of years before: 'Make You Notice'. It was all about a girl trying to get some attention (from a boy who was ignoring her), which fitted in with the theme of the musical: wanting to be famous. It was a song with attitude, which made Michelle feel sassy and confident when she sang it. Sunny had found the music on the Internet, and Jess had recorded her mum playing it on the piano so Michelle could have a practice tape.

'When I get to the part that goes ". . . out of my *head* when you *walk* by", I can do a little jump to the right and put my head on one side,' she said, giving a demonstration.

'You don't want to crick your neck,' Jess said, making the others burst out laughing. 'No, I'm serious!' she went on. 'And jumping around like that makes your hair flop over your face.'

'I'm going to tie it back in a high ponytail,' Michelle said, scooping up her hair. 'What do you think? And I'm going to wear my stretchy flares and a crop top. That won't look too tacky, will it?' She didn't wait for an answer. 'OK, so maybe I'll step to the side instead of jumping and tip my head just a little way over. For the rest of the song I'll stay quite still, apart from moving my arm around. And then when it comes to ". . . and you'll see *me*", I stretch my arm out like this and then make a fist and pull it down to finish. That's what Candy used to do.'

She perched on the end of the bench again, hands on the knee of her outstretched leg. 'Or I could sing a song from the Abba show, I suppose. But Tiffany's doing "Dancing Queen" and I don't want to look like I'm copying her.'

'For the last time! Stick with "Make You Notice",' Caz said. 'It sounds great, and you must have practised it enough times.' And then she was interrupted by the bell: it was time for afternoon school.

'Hey, we haven't talked about the sleepover at my house tomorrow,' Sunny said as they started wandering back to the classrooms. 'No one's forgotten about it, have they?'

'You're not expecting me to come, are you?' Michelle asked – and then realized from Sunny's expression that this was exactly what she *had* been expecting. 'Oh, Sunny – I'm sorry,' she went on. 'There's no way I can make it! Mum's taking me round to Tiffany's house really early on Saturday morning and I have to get a good night's sleep first. You can understand that, can't you?'

'I suppose so,' Sunny said after a pause. 'But you might have told me before now! You know I'm going away on Sunday. It was our one chance to get together, all five of us.'

'We were going to talk about my party,' Jess added. 'Remember? For my birthday that's coming up next week?'

There was an awkward silence. 'Maybe we could we have the sleepover on Saturday night instead,' Caz suggested. 'Would you be back from London in time, Miche?'

'I think so – yes,' Michelle nodded. 'The audition's in the morning, so I'm sure we would. That's a good idea.'

'I'll have to ask Mum,' Sunny said. 'It

depends how early we're leaving on Sunday, I suppose.'

'And that way, I can tell you all how my audition went!' Michelle was buzzing now. 'Yeah, let's make the sleepover for Saturday. That would be so much better!'

'Better for you, maybe,' Sunny said under her breath.

But Michelle was already hurrying on ahead and didn't hear.

'Bye, love,' Yvonne said, scooping Michelle up into a big hug. She added in a whisper, 'You know how proud I am of you – no matter what happens.'

Michelle nodded, a big lump in her throat. After a restless night – full of anxiety dreams about being late for the audition and then discovering her skirt was tucked into her knickers halfway through the song and everyone was pointing at her and laughing – Saturday morning had finally arrived. Her mother had taken her round to Tiffany's house on the way to work and Mrs Wells was going to drive both girls down to London.

Of course, Michelle wished like crazy that *her* mum could have taken her to the audition, but

Yvonne hadn't been able to rearrange her appointments at such short notice. She was a beauty therapist in a big department store, with a lot of customers who asked for her by name. So Tiffany's mother had kindly offered to give Michelle a lift this morning – and she'd better be grateful. That's what Yvonne said, anyway.

Now they were off. 'How's your throat, Tiffany?' Mrs Wells asked as they drove along, shooting her daughter an anxious look. 'Not feeling too tight? Or sore? Would you like a cough pastille? And stop yawning – you know it's bad for your voice.'

'I'm fine,' Tiffany replied sharply. 'Do stop fussing, Mummy! You're only making me feel worse.'

Michelle could tell that Tiffany was just as nervous as she was; she'd hardly said a word on the journey so far and she kept fiddling with the top of her water bottle. Mrs Wells certainly wasn't helping: she kept droning on about what an amazing opportunity this was and how the girls needed to 'shift into top gear' straight away. They'd only have a few minutes to impress the

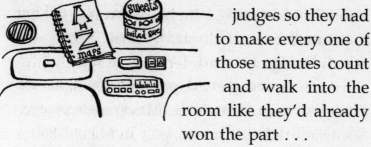

judges so they had to make every one of those minutes count and walk into the room like they'd already won the part . . .

Of course, all of this was really addressed to Tiffany. Michelle sat in the back of the Wells' swanky Range Rover and looked quietly out of the window, letting all the audition advice wash over her head. She'd never been in such a massive car! It felt great to be sitting up so high, looking down on everyone else – as though she was a celebrity already. The feeling that she was about to burst into tears had gone now, thank goodness, but she still had a major attack of the jitters. What if her voice let her down? Singing wasn't like playing the piano. It was more personal than that: something that came from inside her which in some ways was beyond her control. If she went to pieces, she could be truly awful . . .

But you're not *going* to go to pieces, Michelle told herself firmly. You'll walk out there and enjoy yourself, just like you did in the Abba show. Oh dear, now Tiffany's mum was talking to her and she hadn't heard a word. 'Sorry?' she asked, leaning forward. 'What was that?'

'I was saying there'd probably be time for some shopping afterwards,' Mrs Wells repeated. 'That's all right with you, isn't it, Michelle?'

'Oh, sure,' she replied. She'd easily be back in time for the sleepover at Sunny's house, even if they shopped till closing time. And Mrs Wells was in the driving seat, so she had to fall in with her plans, didn't she?

Michelle sat back in her seat again, wondering how she might be feeling 'afterwards'. It was something she hadn't considered before; she'd been too busy thinking about the audition itself. Ella had said they were going to tell all the girls there and then whether they wanted to call them back or not. What if Tiffany got through and she didn't? That would be so awful!

For the next hour or so, Michelle couldn't help pondering over this and other equally terrible possibilities. And then she noticed Tiffany's mother flipping over the pages of a London street map while the car was stopped at a red traffic light. Now the butterflies in her stomach started tap-dancing in hobnailed boots. They must be approaching the rehearsal rooms . . .

'Can you believe it? Look at all these people!' Tiffany stared round the crowded hall. It was jam-packed with girls and their mothers or fathers or older sisters, or whoever else had brought them. There were only just enough folding chairs in the room to give everyone a seat. Michelle had started counting but soon gave up: there must have been about sixty other hopefuls there, besides herself and Tiffany.

When they'd arrived at the rehearsal rooms, their names had been checked off against a list and they'd each been given a number: Tiffany was 54 and Michelle was 57. 'Must be in alphabetical order,' Tiffany said tersely, as they followed the signs to the room where they were supposed to wait for their turn. (She was Tiffany Wells and Michelle was Michelle Williams, so that made sense.)

Coming face to face with the girls she was up against made Michelle feel even more nervous.

So many of them looked really confident and professional – like that dark-haired girl in a super-short mini and leg warmers doing stretches by the window. Or the blonde one sitting next to them, casually eating a sandwich as though she didn't have a care in the world. Or the girl in a 'Cats' T-shirt and leggings who just sat there quietly and watched everybody else, while the smart woman in a business suit beside her talked intently into a mobile phone.

'I bet we're just as good as any of them,' Tiffany said quietly in Michelle's ear.

'Dead right,' she replied, hoping she sounded braver than she felt. It was funny, really: even though she didn't particularly like Tiffany, Michelle was still glad she was there. Of course Jess or Sunny, Caz or Lauren would have been a lot more fun, but at least she had someone her age for company. Most of the girls on their own looked too nervous to try and make friends – if they caught anybody's eye, they glanced away quickly so as not to seem like they were staring.

Now the only thing to do was wait. And wait . . .

After twenty minutes or so, the same man who'd checked them all in appeared at the doorway and called through the first group of girls: numbers one to twenty. Michelle looked at Tiffany and pulled a face – there was a long way to go before they reached the fifties. Why couldn't she be called Michelle Abbott, or Michelle Aardvark? It would have been much better to get her turn over and done with. The air was thick with tension and she felt as though it might suffocate her before long.

Mrs Wells started giving Tiffany another lecture: don't fidget, stand up straight, breathe from your diaphragm, look the judges in the eye, smile all the time . . .

Suddenly Michelle couldn't bear it any longer. 'I'm just going to the loo,' she announced, pushing back her chair. With a bit of luck, she could lock herself away and practise 'Make You Notice' one last time.

But of course everyone had had the same idea, and the toilets were completely full. Michelle squeezed inside, smiling nervously at the auburn-haired girl in the queue in front of her. She looked a bit like Jess, which immediately made Michelle feel better.

'Hiya,' the girl said, smiling back. 'Terrible, isn't it? What number are you?'

'57,' Michelle replied, and the girl groaned sympathetically. 'Tough luck. You're even later than me.'

'I've never been to an audition before,' Michelle confided, as the girl seemed so friendly. 'Have you? D'you know what it's like once you get in there?'

'We've been to a few,' she replied. 'We're at stage school, so we get to hear about them. I'm Katie, by the way. And this is my friend Jo.'

The girl beside her nodded, her face pale and sweaty. 'I think I'm going to throw up,' she muttered, putting a hand over her mouth.

'Don't worry, she always says that but she

never does,' Katie whispered to Michelle. 'Well, she hasn't so far, anyway. This waiting's the worst part – it gets better once you start singing. I've been to one of Richard's auditions before and he's really nice. Have you brought some sheet music for the pianist?'

Michelle felt a leap of panic, even though she must have checked her bag twenty times. The music *had* to be there! She nodded.

'I've brought a backing tape,' said a girl further up the queue, turning round with a very smug expression. This unleashed a buzz of nervous questions from everyone else. Did you really need a backing tape? Could you sing unaccompanied? What if the pianist couldn't play the song you'd chosen? Or played it too fast? Or too slow?

'Don't worry,' Katie told Michelle quietly. 'I bet they won't let her use that tape anyway. They want to hear your voice, not some fancy backing track.' She smiled reassuringly and added, 'Look, are you on your own? Why don't you come and sit with us for a while when you're through here and we'll tell you what we know.'

Ten minutes later, Michelle felt as though

she'd known Katie for ages. Luckily, back in the waiting room Tiffany and her mother had started up a conversation with the blonde girl and her father sitting next to them. Michelle waved to show them where she was, but they hardly seemed to notice. Jo and Katie's mothers were chatting away like old friends (which they probably were), while Katie gave Michelle a few more tips about what to expect and pointed out some girls she knew from the audition circuit. The dark-haired girl in leg warmers was called Sidonie. She went to their stage school and could dance really well, though her voice was nothing special. And the girl in the 'Cats' T-shirt was Sarah Liebermann, who'd starred in the musical 'Annie' – she was brilliant at everything and she already had an agent, who was with her today.

Jo and Katie were both called for their auditions now (they were in the second group), so Michelle wished them both luck and went back to sit with Tiffany and her mother. Mrs Wells was still talking to her neighbour (about stage schools) and Tiffany was grilling his blonde daughter (about her voice coach).

Michelle tried not to listen. She breathed deeply to steady her nerves, and passed the time thinking about comforting things like her mum, and her cats, and her friends at home, and how Ella had told her she sang beautifully and Richard had agreed.

And then, all too soon – even though she'd been waiting a hundred years – the man with the clipboard was calling for 'Numbers 40 through 59 to the audition hall, please – this is the final group,' and she and Tiffany and several other girls dotted around the room were getting to their feet and making their way like sleepwalkers to the door . . .

The audition hall was smaller than the waiting room across the corridor, quieter and more purposeful. Richard sat behind a table next to a youngish woman wearing funky black-framed glasses, whom he introduced to them all as Jackie, and another man was waiting to play the piano. Apart from that, the room was empty – except for some more folding chairs.

To begin with, they all sang a few scales to warm up their voices before starting on the individual audition pieces. Each person had to perform in front of the rest of the group as well as Richard and Jackie. Michelle felt sorry for the girl going first, who would have to sing without the faintest idea what anyone else was like. She looked quite nondescript, too, with mousy

38

brown shoulder-length hair and braces on her teeth. But when she began her number – an old Beatles song called 'Here, There and Everywhere' – the sound of her voice was so incredibly sweet and clear that Michelle felt as though she might burst into tears. She caught Tiffany's eye and they raised eyebrows at each other; this would be a hard act to follow.

The next few girls weren't nearly so good, then came two who were great, and then it was Sidonie's turn – Miss Legwarmers 1977, as Michelle had privately christened her. She struck a dramatic pose to start, head bowed down and hands behind her back, and danced throughout her song before finishing with the splits as a grand finale. It didn't quite work, though; Sidonie seemed to be putting more energy into her complicated routine than her singing. And while she was obviously a great gymnast, she was nowhere near hitting some of the high notes. Michelle decided there and then to concentrate on her voice and keep the background movements to a minimum.

A little while after Sidonie, Tiffany took her place near the piano. She looked very composed and confident, standing there with one foot turned out neatly and a big smile on her face. Just as well parents aren't allowed in here, Michelle thought, or her mother would probably be hissing out instructions right now. Not that Tiffany needed any reminders: she stood up straight, didn't fidget, looked at the judges, and turned in a great performance. Mrs Wells would have been proud.

'Well done!' Michelle said, when Tiffany came back to her seat and everyone else was applauding (as they had for each turn). 'You were brilliant!'

The girl who came next was so awful that Michelle could hardly bear to listen. Her legs were shaking and her voice was so flat that it was amazing she'd got into the audition in the first place. Of course they all clapped just the same – poor thing, she must have realized she'd messed up – and for the girl after her, who wasn't very good either. And then it was Michelle's turn.

The strangest thing happened as she stood by the piano and smiled at Richard and Jackie. Suddenly, it was as though she remembered what she was doing there in the first place – what this audition was all about. The nervous energy that had been unsettling her until now gathered itself up into one great surge of power, and everybody else in the room seemed to disappear except for the two judges. She knew beyond the shadow of a doubt that she would sing 'Make You Notice' like she'd never sung it before. This was her moment, and she was going to make the most of it!

'This is ridiculous! Why on earth do they have to keep us waiting so long?' Mrs Wells put down her half-eaten sandwich and stood up, bristling with indignation. 'I'm going to have another word with that young man. He is meant to be organizing this shambles, after all.'

'Don't Mummy, please! Sit down – people are looking!' Tiffany was bright red with embarrassment, and Michelle didn't blame her. Mrs Wells kept complaining about the 'facilities' at the top of her voice, and she'd already demanded to know how much longer the judges would need to reach a decision. Surely she could see that kicking up a fuss like this wouldn't make the slightest bit of difference?

The last group to audition – Michelle and Tiffany's – had come back to the waiting room about half an hour before, and now everyone was eating (or trying to eat) a sandwich lunch while they waited to hear who was going on to the next round of auditions. At last, when everybody's nerves were stretched to breaking point, Richard and Jackie appeared in the doorway. Immediately, you could have heard a pin drop.

Richard spoke first, about what a difficult decision it had been and how they'd have liked to give everyone a part ('I bet he always says that,' Tiffany whispered to Michelle), and then announced that Jackie would read out a list of numbers. If your number was called, please could you go through to the audition hall when Jackie had finished speaking. If your number was *not* on the list, then he was afraid you hadn't got through – but thanks very much for coming anyway, and better luck next time. And could everyone stay as quiet as possible, so that Jackie could be heard.

Michelle stared down at her hands, clenched tightly in her lap. Don't cry, whatever you do, she told herself sternly. If your number's not there, it won't be the end of the world.

Jackie started reading out the lucky numbers, slowly and clearly. A couple of people couldn't resist a quiet exclamation under their breath but, for the most part, the room stayed calm. One girl burst into tears when she realized her number hadn't been called, but she managed to cry without making too much noise.

'. . . 34 . . . 37 . . . 39 . . .'

Nearly there. Michelle's heart was beating so loudly she thought everyone else must be able to hear it too.

'. . . 40 . . .' So the girl with the beautiful voice had got through. Well, that was no surprise.

'. . . 46 . . . 48 . . . 49 . . . 54 . . .' And so had Tiffany! Michelle didn't know whether to be pleased or not. She gave Tiffany a quick smile, for form's sake, but Mrs Wells was already hugging her close so she didn't see. And Sidonie was out! The splits hadn't been enough to save her.

Oh, for heaven's sake! Why was Michelle bothering about Sidonie at a time like this? There was only one number she should be concentrating on, and that was . . .

'. . . 57 . . .' Jackie called – and Michelle let out her breath in a great big rush and felt her shoulders slump with relief. Yes! She'd done it! They were through to the next round, she and Tiffany together.

Michelle suddenly knew that if Tiffany had passed and she hadn't, she couldn't have borne it. But how could she put herself through all this a second time? And possibly a third, after that? You'll just have to learn to cope with it, she said to herself, giving Tiffany a genuine grin this time and a thumbs-up signal. That's what show business is all about . . .

'Can you believe this is really happening?' Michelle looked at Tiffany across the café table, her eyes sparkling. They were sitting outside in the middle of Covent Garden, listening to a jazz group busking on the pavement nearby and drinking fruit smoothies. The bright afternoon was gradually fading into a warm, dusky evening, and there were loads of shops all around them still open for browsing. (Mrs Wells was buying some luscious bath things right now.) Paradise!

Best of all, tucked safely in her pocket were the words and music for a song from the show. When all the successful applicants had gone back through to the audition hall that afternoon, a choreographer was waiting for them. She and Mac, the pianist, were going to teach the girls a number that they'd have to perform at the next audition on Wednesday. But first of all, she told them some more about the musical. It was going to be called 'Shooting Stars'. They might not have known the director's name – Jody Marshall – but she was one of the most successful pop song-writers ever. A couple of years ago, she'd had an idea for a musical, and she'd been writing material for it ever since. There were some brilliant new songs, which would probably be released as singles after the show had opened.

Of course, that made everyone even more excited than ever. There were about twenty-five girls left. Michelle saw several she recognized from the waiting room: Sarah Leibermann in her 'Cats' T-shirt, the blonde girl who'd sat next to them and chatted with Tiffany, and ginger-haired Katie, who was smiling at her and waving. There was no sign of her friend, Jo.

First of all, Mac took them through the song: 'Step by Step'. The lyrics had been written up on a flip chart at the front of the room, and he played the music and sang it through for them a couple of times. When their turn came, they were a little hesitant to begin with, but Mac soon had them all 'singing out', as he called it. The song was great, really catchy and upbeat. At first Michelle had some trouble with the final note, which was quite high for her and had to be held for a long time, but once she relaxed and breathed properly, she found it much easier to sing. And then Bet, the choreographer, took them through the dance routine. It was so difficult to remember everything! You had to concentrate all the time to have any chance of ending up in the right place, on the right beat.

'OK,' Bet said eventually. 'That'll do for now. But I want you to go away and practise, practise, *practise*, so it's perfect for the next audition on Wednesday. The harder you work, the better your chances of getting through to the final one.'

But they deserved some relaxation time first, Michelle reasoned, and so did Tiffany. So here they were in the café.

'I'm glad you got through as well,' Tiffany said. 'It's much more fun with the two of us, isn't it? And maybe we could practise together round at my house.'

'Sure,' Michelle agreed. 'That would be fab.' Tiffany was being so nice! She couldn't help wondering whether she'd misjudged her in the past. Perhaps it was just that they'd never really got to know each other outside the Saturday drama group. They'd certainly had a great time together this afternoon, wandering round the shops and giggling at some of the super trendy people.

'Just imagine if we were both in the show!' Michelle sighed. 'Wouldn't it be brilliant? We could share the travelling together, or maybe stay in London overnight sometimes.' She'd hardly dared let herself think about being chosen for the musical before now. It would only make things worse if she didn't get through.

'We *will* be in that show!' Tiffany said, leaning across the table. 'That's how you have to think. If you want something badly enough, you'll get it – that's what my father says, and he's right. I'll do anything to get one of those parts! Anything.'

Michelle was taken aback by the strength of feeling in her voice. 'Yeah, me too,' she said, thinking her words sounded rather feeble in comparison.

Tiffany looked at her. 'This is a big thing for us,' she said. 'You realize that, don't you? It's like the start of our career.' And then she smiled. 'We ought to celebrate! I went to this amazing Japanese restaurant quite near here for my birthday last year. Why don't we go ask my mum to take us there tonight? Yours won't mind, will she? You can ring up again and tell her about it.'

(Michelle had already borrowed Mrs Well's mobile phone to tell her mother she'd got through the audition.)

'Sorry, I can't,' Michelle said apologetically. 'I'm meant to be going to a sleepover round at my friend's house.'

Tiffany dismissed this with a wave of her hand. 'Oh, you can have a boring old sleepover any time. This evening is special, and we're in London! Let's not waste it going straight home.' She drained her smoothie and added, 'Besides, *I* want to go and my mum's driving the car, so you'll have to come along. You'll love this place! The chef juggles with knives and it's really cool. We'll have so much fun.'

Michelle did feel a twinge of guilt, but it soon passed. Home seemed a million miles away and anyway, Tiffany was right: Michelle couldn't start ordering Mrs Wells around like she was a taxi driver. Her friends would understand . . .

It was late when Mrs Wells dropped Michelle back home that night, and later still by the time she'd told her mother all about the audition and everything that had happened afterwards.

'So the next one's on Wednesday,' Yvonne said. 'Perfect! I'm not working that day, so I can take you along – and Tiffany as well, if she likes. We'll go on the train, though. I hate driving in London.'

'Oh, I expect Tiffany'll probably want to go with her mum,' Michelle said quickly. Somehow, she didn't think the idea of public transport would appeal to her; it wouldn't be half as comfortable as swishing along in the Range Rover.

'I think we ought to offer, at least,' Yvonne

said. 'After all, it is our turn. I'll give Mrs Wells a ring tomorrow and see what she says.'

'Whatever,' Michelle yawned. Suddenly, she felt exhausted. It even seemed too much of an effort to get out of the chair, drag her feet along the corridor and flop into bed. Pity she was too big for a piggy-back.

'You've both done brilliantly to get through,' her mother said again, giving her another hug. 'Well done!' She reached out an arm to pull Michelle up. 'And now it's time for your beauty sleep.'

When Michelle was finally tucked up in bed, her mum made a space for herself to sit down at the end of the mattress. Michelle could tell from the look on her face that she had something serious to say. 'I know you're tired,' she began, 'but we need to talk some time about you missing Sunny's sleepover.'

'What about it?' Michelle mumbled. All she wanted to do now was fall asleep.

'Sunny was really disappointed,' Yvonne said.

'I could tell from her voice. And quite cross, too. I didn't realize they'd rearranged the whole thing for tonight just so you could be there, Michelle!'

'Look, it wasn't my fault, was it?' Michelle sat up indignantly, wide awake now. 'Tiffany and her mum both wanted to go to this restaurant. I could hardly tell them not to, could I? They were being so nice to me – Mrs Wells bought me that lovely bath bomb and everything. What was I supposed to say? "Sorry, you have to take me straight home because I need to get back for a sleepover." Hardly!'

'All right, calm down.' Yvonne patted her feet. 'I can see it must have been difficult. Just don't forget how your old friends might be feeling, that's all. It might be tactful not to talk about the audition *too* much over the next few days. I mean, imagine if it was one of them going off to London all the time! You'd probably be a little bit jealous, wouldn't you?'

'I wasn't jealous when Jess won that competition and went backstage at the roadshow,' Michelle said obstinately, lying back down on her pillow. 'Not really, anyway – and she even

52

ended up on TV! Well, now it's my turn. I think I know my friends better than you do. They're cool about all this, trust me.'

'I hope you're right,' her mother said, getting up to turn off the light. 'And there's no need to be rude.'

Michelle lay there in the darkness, fuming. OK, she might have gone slightly over the top, but her mother was way off the mark this time! Sunny was bound to realize there was nothing she could have done about getting to the sleep-over on time and, to be honest, Michelle couldn't see why she was making such a fuss about it. Surely Sunny could see she had slightly more important things on her mind at the moment?

In fact, Michelle didn't know why she was bothering to get herself in a state right now. Because you should have made more of an effort, said a nagging little voice somewhere inside her head. You should have rung Sunny yourself. And you should have been more disappointed about missing the sleepover than you were. You wanted to go to the restaurant instead, didn't you? So you didn't really care about letting your friends down, and that's not very nice.

Michelle put her hands over her ears and turned over, determined not to listen any more. She'd make it up to Sunny tomorrow. Hey, maybe if she got a part in the show she could get all her friends tickets for a special box or something! And when it was time for the curtain call she'd come out on stage and give them a big wave so they'd know how much she appreciated them . . .

Thinking these lovely thoughts, she drifted happily off to sleep.

The next morning, Michelle slept till past eleven o'clock. She woke up to see sunlight streaming through her curtains and lay in bed for a while, dozing in the warmth. A delicious smell of fresh coffee seeped through the flat: her mother always made a pot on Sundays and drank it while she read the papers. Why can't coffee taste as good as it smells, Michelle wondered sleepily to herself. She

54

preferred a cup of tea. In fact, a cup of tea was just what she fancied right now. Throwing back the duvet, she got out of bed and padded off to find her mother in the kitchen. They hadn't parted on very good terms last night, and she owed her an apology for being so lippy.

'That's all right,' Yvonne said, when Michelle had made her peace. 'I know you were tired, and I probably shouldn't have talked to you about it last night. But you will ring Sunny this morning, won't you, love? Try and speak to her before she goes away.'

'OK.' Michelle yawned and stretched her arms luxuriously. 'After I've had a cup of tea. And some breakfast. I'm starving!' The Japanese restaurant last night might have looked fantastic (indoor pools full of giant fish and stepping stones across to reach the low tables) but the food was very peculiar. Raw fish was hardly her idea of a slap-up meal.

Two mugs of tea and a plate of bacon and eggs later, Michelle was ready to tackle Sunny. I'll tell her how sorry I am and invite her round for a sleepover here, she thought, dialling the Kumars' number. The answerphone was on, though; they must have left already. Michelle felt guiltily relieved. Sunny would have a great time visiting her cousins and by the time she came back, she'd have cooled down a little. Still, maybe it would be a good idea to ring Jess and find out what they'd decided about her birthday party. She could tell her all about the audition, too.

Jess sounded distinctly cool on the phone. 'Oh, hello,' she said. 'What happened to you last night?'

'I couldn't get back in time,' Michelle replied, slightly surprised by her tone of voice. Did she have to apologize to each of her friends in turn? 'Tiffany wanted to go to this Japanese restaurant, so we stayed in London. Sorry, but there wasn't anything I could do about it. Did you have a good time?'

'Yeah, it was fine,' Jess said – and that was it. Michelle waited for her to ask, 'And what about you? How did the audition go? Did you get through?' but the questions never came. Just an awkward pause which she had to fill.

'Well?' she prompted Jess eventually. 'Don't you want to know how I got on yesterday?'

'Sure. How did you get on yesterday?' Jess asked, still in that distant, casual voice which implied she didn't really care.

'They've asked us to come back for the next audition!' Michelle told her. Surely Jess would drum up some enthusiasm when she heard *that*! 'Me and Tiffany. We've got a number from the show to learn and we have to perform it on Wednesday.'

'Great. Well done,' Jess said. 'So that practice tape we made was a help, then?'

'Of course it was,' Michelle said, starting to feel irritated. Why was Jess behaving like this? All because she missed one sleepover! Couldn't her friends manage without her for one evening? 'Say thanks to your mum for me, won't you? And tell her I got through?'

'Why don't you tell her yourself?' Jess replied. 'She's right here. I'll pass you over.'

'Jess! What's up with you?' Michelle exploded. 'Is it really such a big deal that I missed the sleepover last night?'

'Well, yes. Since you ask, actually it *is* a big deal,' Jess snapped back. 'If we'd known you weren't going to pitch up, we'd have kept the sleepover on Friday night. That would have been a lot more convenient for Sunny – and for me, as it happens. Claire had two of her stupid friends round on Friday and I did *not* want to be at home.' (Claire was Jess's older sister – they didn't get on very well.)

'Honestly, Miche,' she went on, 'Mum and I spent ages recording that tape and you've hardly bothered to say thank you! And what about the card Lauren made for you? The one we all signed?'

'What about it?' Michelle stammered, caught on the back foot. Lauren had made her a wonderful good luck card, covered in green tissue paper four-leafed clovers and with a pop-up black cat inside. She'd meant to take it with her to the audition, but it must be still in her school bag somewhere.

'Haven't you wondered where it is?' Jess asked. 'Well, don't bother – I'll tell you. Caz and Lauren found it in the playground on

58

Friday, after you'd gone home, all muddy and spoilt.'

'Oh no! It must have fallen out of my bag.' Now Michelle felt terrible. 'It was a great card! I loved it, really I did.'

'Well you didn't take much care of it, did you?' Jess didn't sound convinced. Still, at least she was talking in her normal voice now.

'I'm sorry,' Michelle said again, and this time she truly meant it. 'I was so nervous before the audition, I just couldn't think straight. Look, can you come over this afternoon? There's nothing I can do about Sunny now, but I'll ring Lauren and say sorry about the card, and ask her and Caz round too. We'll have a lovely girly time and I won't talk about the audition, I promise. Oh, please, Jess – say you'll come! I hate it when you're cross with me like this.'

There was a pause. Then, to Michelle's relief, Jess eventually said, 'All right, but you'd better keep that promise! If you start yakking on about the show, I'm going home.'

'I won't, believe me,' Michelle assured her.

Everything's going to be fine, she thought,

hanging up the phone. She'd patch things up with Lauren and then this afternoon she'd make the flat really cozy with loads of scented candles and music and her mum could give them all manicures. Things would be just like they used to be before she'd ever heard of 'Shooting Stars', and she wouldn't mention it – or sing, either.

Well, maybe if her friends *had* truly forgiven her, she could quickly go through 'Step by Step' with the dance routine so they could tell her what they thought. But only once. And only if they really didn't mind . . .

'Your mum's so neat,' Lauren sighed, looking at her hands with great satisfaction. 'I love these designs!'

Yvonne had given her chequerboard nails – red with rows of tiny black squares. She had a special little brush with about three hairs in it for really fiddly patterns like this, and she'd given them each a different look. Caz had a star on each finger and a crescent moon on her thumbnails, while Michelle's nails were white with black cowprint patches. Now the beauty session was over, they were all chilling out in the big kitchen-cum-living-room at the heart of the flat. Yvonne had just gone out for a quick run, but nobody else had felt energetic enough to join her.

'And there's no school next week, so we can

keep the varnish on as long as we like,' Michelle said. 'Good idea of mine, don't you think?'

It was such a relief to feel they were all friends again! Lauren had taken quite a lot of talking round on the phone. But eventually, after Michelle had spent ages explaining and grovelled quite a bit too, she'd lost the same frosty tone that had been in Jess's voice and agreed to come over that afternoon. The next phone call wasn't quite so difficult. When Caz realized how sorry Michelle was for the way things had turned out, she'd forgiven her straight away.

And now Michelle was going to be super-nice, to make up for everything! Although she'd promised not to talk about the audition, she couldn't do anything about that well of excitement bubbling up inside her except let it spill over and share it around. Of course she didn't want to make anyone feel resentful about all the great things that were happening to her, but it was difficult to hide how happy she felt. She loved everyone! Even Tiffany, who'd rung up earlier that day to invite her round so they could practise together.

'Who wants a smoothie?' she asked, scrambling up from the squashy sofa. 'We've got some strawberries in the fridge.' The drinks she and Tiffany had shared yesterday were so delicious, she wanted to try making some herself.

'I'll help you,' Lauren offered, and they soon had the liquidizer whirring. When the four tall glasses on a tray had been filled, everyone drank quietly for a while, busy with their own thoughts. They'd known each other for such a long time, there was no need to make conversation. Michelle, of course, was running through the lyrics to 'Step by Step' in her head. Well, she might have been singing them out loud – but only very quietly.

Jess, Lauren and Caz exchanged glances. 'OK, Miche,' Caz said, putting her empty glass down on the table. 'I suppose you'd better tell us what happened yesterday. It's the only thing on your mind, isn't it?'

'Sorry, sorry,' Michelle said guiltily – though she couldn't help feeling slightly irritated too. Of course it was the only thing on her mind! The others'd be just the same, wouldn't they?

Anyway, they listened attentively while she told them all about the audition and then they even let her perform 'Step by Step' and told her she'd looked OK afterwards.

'We have to sing it on Wednesday, in front of some more people from the company,' Michelle said, slumping into a chair. 'And if we get through that, the final audition's on Saturday. In the actual theatre, in front of the director!'

'It would be,' Jess groaned. 'Our party's on Saturday – mine and Matt's.' (Matt was Jess's twin brother.) 'That's what we decided last night, even though it's not our birthday till Monday.'

'Are you having another disco?' Michelle asked, hoping the answer would be yes. Jess and Matt had had a brilliant disco for their birthday last year. And if the party was in the evening, she'd have time to get there after the audition.

'Sort of,' Jess replied. 'There isn't time to organize anything major, but we're going to clear all the furniture out of the living room and have a seventies party. Most of Matt's friends are around and I've rung some of the girls in our class.

64

Everyone's going to dress up in glitter and platform shoes and there'll be loads of disco music to dance to.'

'Oh, cool!' That would suit Michelle just fine – especially if she could borrow Trish's skirt and boots again.

'It was your Abba show that gave us the idea,' Lauren explained.

'And beforehand, in the afternoon, Mum's taking us to check out that new swimming pool,' Jess added. 'Because Matt's going to be round at Jamie's house all day.'

Michelle thought over her schedule. 'Look, I probably won't be called back on Saturday anyway,' she said. 'But if I do, would it be OK if I just came for the party in the evening? And this time I promise to be there – even if I have to walk the whole way!'

Surely Jess couldn't object to that?

Luckily, she didn't. 'Of course it's OK,' she said. 'Come on, d'you think I'd expect you to turn this audition down? Just so long as you realize my party matters too. Maybe not so much, but it matters all the same.'

'Sure, I know.' Michelle nodded: she could understand that.

'Are you doing anything tomorrow?' Caz asked. 'We thought we'd go bowling.'

'Oh, sorry – I'm going round to Tiffany's to practise for the audition,' Michelle said without thinking. 'But I'm free on Tuesday,' she added quickly. 'Let's go out then! Perhaps Mum can take us shopping, or maybe we could go to the cinema or something. I'll give you a ring in the morning and we can fix it up.'

Everyone seemed to think that was a good idea, much to Michelle's relief. Phew! She didn't want her friends thinking she'd sooner spend time with Tiffany than with them . . .

The next morning, Michelle's mum dropped her round at Tiffany's house for the rehearsal

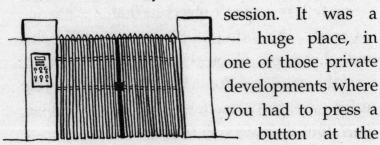

session. It was a huge place, in one of those private developments where you had to press a button at the electric gates for someone inside to open them up and let you in. While Yvonne talked to Mrs Wells about the travel arrangements for Wednesday, Tiffany took Michelle through the house to a large airy room overlooking the back garden with a piano at the far end. A series of full-length mirrors ran all the way along the opposite wall.

'This is the music room,' she announced matter-of-factly. 'It's great for dancing too, because you can watch yourself and see what you're doing wrong.'

'Perfect,' Michelle said, gazing around. The room was enormous! In fact, you could probably have fitted their whole flat inside it. 'Do you play the piano?' she asked. 'I've always wanted to learn.'

Oh yeah? Since when? That voice inside her head had started up again.

'I've just started,' Tiffany replied. 'It's my mother's piano, mainly – she's really good. She used to work in the theatre, you know.'

'Fine! Everything's settled for Wednesday.' Bang on cue, Tiffany's mother came sweeping into the room and sat down at the piano stool.

'Of course I wish I could come too, but Fergus is entertaining clients for lunch and he needs me there to oil the wheels. Thank goodness your mother was free, Michelle.'

'Oh, right.' Michelle couldn't think of anything else to say. Mrs Wells made her feel drained, somehow: she had such a loud booming voice and she was so bossy and definite about the way everything ought to be done. Like a big blonde steamroller.

'Fergus is my father,' Tiffany told her, 'in case you were wondering. He's a business consultant.'

'Oh, is he?' Michelle said, trying to sound interested and hoping Tiffany wasn't going to start asking embarrassing questions about *her* father (who had gone off when she was a baby and didn't feature in her life at all). Luckily she didn't.

'Now let's get down to work.' Mrs Wells turned to the piano and started flexing her fingers, ready to play. 'We'll run through the song a couple of times on its own first and then you can add the dance routine. Tiffany, be sure to remember everything I told you yesterday.'

They'd obviously done a lot of work on 'Step by Step' already. Michelle had to look at her songsheet a few times to remind herself of the lyrics, but Tiffany was word perfect. She had to be! Her mother was so hard to please, taking them through the same phrases over and over again until she was quite satisfied with the way they were singing. 'You must fill the theatre with sound!' she kept saying. 'Project your voice! You need to reach people sitting right in the very back row. But enunciate clearly! I want to hear every word. And look happy, for goodness' sake!'

After half an hour, Michelle's head was spinning. She was so busy trying to enunciate and project and smile at the same time, she didn't know whether she was coming or going.

'Can't we stop now, Mummy?' Tiffany was obviously feeling the same. 'We don't want to strain our voices and I'm sure Michelle's had enough. Haven't you, Michelle?'

'Well, maybe,' she replied, not wanting to offend anyone. 'Perhaps we should start practising our dance moves?'

'All right,' Mrs Wells said. 'That's fine by me.

I'll play the music while you go through the routine.'

'It's OK,' Tiffany told her, 'we'll use the tape. Why don't you let us rehearse on our own for a while now?'

'But how will you know what you're doing wrong?' Mrs Wells sounded quite put out. 'It's always better to perform in front of an audience.'

'We can see ourselves in the mirror,' Tiffany said. 'Please, Mummy! It'll be fine with just the two of us.'

'Oh, all right,' her mother said, gathering herself up from the piano. 'If you insist. But I'll come back in half an hour or so and see how you're getting on.'

Michelle had been wondering why Tiffany had asked her over in the first place; now she was beginning to understand. She needed an ally, someone to take her side against her mother.

Things were much more relaxed now Mrs Wells wasn't around, though the two girls worked just as hard. Tiffany had a tape of the music to 'Step by Step' (played by her mother, Michelle guessed) and they practised the dance routine until it was much smoother. At first, Michelle felt quite self-conscious about watching herself in the mirror, but it really did help her see where she needed to improve. Her turns had to be tighter, and her arms were way too loose and floppy at the moment.

'Well done, girls!' Mrs Wells said, coming into the music room followed by a girl who looked about their age, carrying a tray of drinks. 'That's coming on very nicely.' She smiled at Michelle. 'It's fun for Tiffany to have a friend to rehearse with, instead of an old fogey like me.'

Michelle wasn't sure whether she'd count Tiffany as a friend yet; after all, they went to different schools and they didn't really have that much in common. But at least she could talk to her for as long as she wanted about music and dance, and what the next audition would be like, without worrying about being boring. She took a glass off the tray and smiled uncertainly at the girl who was carrying it, not sure whether she was a friend of Tiffany's.

'Rula's our au pair,' Tiffany explained casually. She drained her glass and plonked it back on the tray for Rula to take away, then stretched out her legs and examined her feet critically. 'These dance shoes are looking so tatty! We're going shopping tomorrow for some more. Do you want to come along? You could do with a new pair too.'

Michelle felt herself blush with embarrassment. Her jazz shoes were in a far worse state than Tiffany's! The soft black leather was all scuffed around the toes, and starting to come away from the sole in one place. But they'd been expensive and they still fitted her, so she hadn't liked to ask her mother for another pair.

'Maybe. I'd better have a word with my mum first,' she replied hesitantly. 'I'm not sure what we're doing tomorrow.'

'But this is important!' Tiffany was quite certain about that. 'If you're not dressed properly, how can you feel confident?'

'Think of it as an investment,' Mrs Wells added. 'You girls have a glittering future ahead of you! As long as you keep working hard, there's no limit to what you can achieve.'

Michelle couldn't help smiling. A glittering future! She liked the sound of that . . .

'Mum, please! Can you stop going on at me all the time?' Michelle hissed across the table separating their train seats. 'Tiffany's going to come back from the buffet any moment now and she'll hear you! Not to mention everyone else in this carriage.'

'All right, all right,' Yvonne said, going back to her book. 'Just so long as you think about what I've said. I don't like to see you treating your friends this way, Michelle – especially after what happened on Saturday.'

'But I've told you a million times, I explained about Saturday!' Now Michelle was really losing patience. 'And it wasn't a definite arrangement for yesterday. I only said *maybe* I'd give Caz a ring and we could fix something up.'

'But you didn't give her a ring, did you?' her mother said, looking up from the page again. 'That's the whole point. If you'd rung the day before to say you were going out with Tiffany, it would have been different. But Caz certainly seemed to think you were all meant to be meeting up yesterday. It looks like you pulled out at the last minute because something better came along.'

'Just drop it, Mum! You don't understand anything.' Michelle couldn't believe the way her mother was hassling her about some casual plan that she might or might not have made. Today of all days, when she had so much else on her mind!

It was Wednesday – audition day – and they were halfway to London on the train. Tiffany had been fine about not going by car, much to Michelle's relief. In fact she seemed much less tense than she had been on Saturday – probably because her mother's not around, Michelle thought to herself. All the same, she did think *her* mother could manage to be a little more excited about what lay ahead, instead of droning on about what had happened yesterday.

The day before, Michelle had managed to persuade her mother that she really did need a new pair of dance shoes (that 'investment' line from Mrs Wells had tipped the balance) and she'd gone off in the morning to buy them with Tiffany and her mum. After that, they'd had lunch in a café and then she and Tiffany had spent some more time rehearsing and talking about the audition. When Michelle had finally come home, her mother passed on Lauren's message but there'd been no time to do anything about it then. Ella, their Saturday voice coach, was due any minute to listen to a run-through of 'Step by Step'. And after Ella had gone, Michelle was so busy thinking about what she'd said that ringing Lauren quite slipped her mind.

'Hold it right there!' Ella had declared when Michelle had come to the end of the first verse. 'Why are you singing like this? What's got into you?'

'I'm trying to project my voice,' Michelle had replied, slightly hurt. 'Don't you think it sounds better?'

'No, I don't!' Ella had been quite sure about that. 'You're going to strain your vocal cords if you carry on like that. Now start again – and this time I want you to *sing* instead of shouting. Relax, breathe deeply, and let that lovely voice of yours come flowing out naturally. You don't have to smile every second, either. It looks really false.'

So basically, Ella had disagreed with everything Tiffany's mother had said. But she *was* a proper singing teacher – despite Mrs Wells' view that she was young and inexperienced. And when she thought about it, Michelle knew she made a much sweeter sound when she sang with Ella than she ever had at Tiffany's house. Smiling all the time was beginning to make her jaw ache, too.

Still, her dancing was a lot better after all that practice. In fact, Michelle was feeling quite confident this morning: at least she knew what to expect now! And her fab new jazz dance shoes lay ready and waiting in her rucksack. Clothes-wise, Ella had told her to wear the same thing to every audition, because that would help the judges to remember her. (Richard certainly ought to recognize her, but the others might need a nudge.) Apparently Ella had been to loads of auditions herself when she was a music student, so she was full of practical advice.

But best of all, today Michelle's mum was with her – and that was bound to bring her luck. She felt on top of the world. How could she possibly fail?

'I knew we'd do it,' Tiffany said, tucking into her cheese roll. 'Didn't you, Michelle?'

'Not really,' she replied through a mouthful of salt-and-vinegar crisps. 'They turned down some excellent people.'

A couple of hours later, it was all over – and both Michelle and Tiffany had got through to the final audition! They'd be coming back to London on Saturday afternoon to perform in front of Jody Marshall, the show's director. So why wasn't Michelle jumping for joy and dancing along the Thames Embankment, where they were sitting on a bench having a picnic?

Tiffany had assumed they'd be going to a

smart café for lunch, but Michelle knew her mother didn't have much money to spare after forking out for the new dance shoes and train fares. Anyway, it was much nicer to eat outside.

Sunlight sparkling on the water turned the river into a sheet of silver and a couple of stray gulls blown in from the sea wheeled above their heads, hoping for crusts. But even that couldn't lift Michelle's mood. What on earth was the matter with her?

She thought back over everything that had happened that morning. The audition had been organized slightly differently this time. Instead of splitting up the girls into smaller groups, they'd all gone through to the hall together. Mac had been sitting by the piano with Bet, the choreographer, in her soft floppy trousers and cross-over ballet top. But there had been several other people waiting to look at them whom Michelle hadn't seen before. All those eyes, trained on her! (And on the others, of course.) Michelle began to feel very self-conscious: as usual, she was by far the tallest girl there.

Today, they'd all worked together, singing and dancing as a group. First of all, they'd performed 'Step by Step', and then Mac had taught them another song from the show. A slow ballad, for a change, to vary the tempo. Some of the judges wandered among the rows of girls, listening to individual voices, and sometimes they asked one person to sing on her own while the others took a break. The girl with braces sang a solo, then a couple of others Michelle vaguely recognized from last time – and then they asked her to sing alone too! It doesn't mean anything, Michelle told herself when she'd finished. But surely that couldn't be a bad sign, could it? She could see Tiffany glowering at her from the sidelines, and that had only made her feel better.

Michelle sighed. The truth of the matter was, she suddenly felt lonely. She'd never been exactly close to Tiffany and the gulf between them was getting wider, the further along the audition road they went. There was something so cold and ruthless about her! She didn't seem to care about anyone or anything, apart from getting a part in this musical. Katie had forgotten her songsheet that morning and asked Michelle if she could borrow hers, to have another look through the 'Step by Step' lyrics. Of course Michelle had gladly lent it (she knew the words backwards by now) – and Tiffany had given her such a hard time about it afterwards!

'You know how many girls they're looking for, don't you?' she'd hissed. 'Nine. There must be nearly thirty here today and we're all competing against each other. What if Katie gets one of those parts and you don't? How would you feel then? If she hasn't bothered to learn the words, that's her lookout.'

'But I like Katie,' Michelle protested. 'She was really nice to me on Saturday.'

'This isn't about being nice,' Tiffany said, narrowing her eyes as she looked round the room. 'It's about winning.'

Well, she and Tiffany had won, and Katie hadn't. Of course Michelle had been over the moon when her number was called out after Tiffany's at the end of the audition, but seeing

Katie look so disappointed had taken the edge off her happiness. It would be a real shame not to have her there at the next audition, too. Katie was so friendly and – normal, somehow. She didn't look at everyone else as if they were her deadliest rivals, like some of the other girls did. Was that really what you had to be like if you wanted to succeed?

Tiffany couldn't stop talking on the journey home but Michelle was quiet, and so was her mother. They picked up the car from the station and dropped Tiffany at her house before going back to the flat.

'What do you think about all this, Mum?' Michelle asked, when they were both sitting in the kitchen and the kettle was boiling for a pot of tea.

Yvonne thought for a while before she answered. 'Look, I don't want to hold you back,' she replied eventually. 'I know you have a talent and you ought to use it, which is why I haven't said anything before now. Maybe I didn't think you'd get so far. But if you are picked for this show, it'll change your life in a big way and that worries me. Not to mention how we're going to manage going to London two or three times a week. It'll be hard enough finding a way to get you there this Saturday afternoon. I'll have to give Tiffany's mum a ring and see if she can take you.'

'Oh, Mum! Can't you get the day off?' Michelle pleaded. 'This *is* quite important!'

'I know,' her mother replied. 'The trouble is, one of my regular clients is getting married on Saturday and I'm meant to be doing her make-up. I'm sorry, but I really can't let her down. You understand that, don't you, love?'

'No,' Michelle said grumpily. 'Tell her to get married on Monday instead.'

'I was talking to your friend Katie's mother this morning,' Yvonne went on, making the tea. 'She's given up her job so she can take Katie to these auditions, and they've moved closer to London to cut down on the travelling. But I can't afford to stop working! And we're so happy here. You'd have to go a long way to find friends like ours.'

That was certainly true. And yet . . . Michelle remembered how excited she'd been when Ella had first told her and Tiffany about the auditions. Maybe there was some way to work it all out. She reached for the biscuits: eating usually helped her to think.

'Perhaps I should talk to Ella about it,' she decided. 'She's acted in a couple of musicals, so she must know more about it than we do.'

'That's a great idea,' her mother said. 'Why not give her a ring?'

Ella had given Michelle her mobile number so that they could talk about how the audition had gone, if she wanted. She dug it out of her pocket and went to find the phone.

'Don't let Tiffany put you off!' Ella's voice crackled cheerfully down the line a few minutes later. 'She's got a bad case of pushy mother syndrome, poor thing. There's no need to be quite so single-minded – especially not at your age. Have some fun at these auditions! And if you do get a part in the show, well, I'm sure the theatre company can work something out to help with the journey. They might even lay on a car and driver for you.'

Wow, celebrity stuff! Michelle couldn't help thinking.

'Don't forget about the rest of your life,' Ella advised. 'School, friends – that all matters too, you know. There are years ahead for everything else!'

Michelle was feeling much happier by the time she hung up. Ella had helped her put things into perspective. Performing could be one part of her life, just like it was now, rather than crowding everything else out like it seemed to do in Tiffany's. Of course she didn't have to drop her closest friends! She was feeling dead tired now, but tomorrow she'd ring round and see what they were up to. A break from rehearsing would probably do her good, anyway . . .

MICHELLE CENTRE STAGE

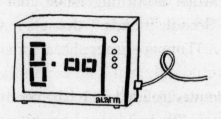

Michelle's mother left early for work on Thursday morning, so she spent most of that day at home with Mrs Shepherd from the flat upstairs keeping an eye on her. She tried calling her friends but none of them seemed to be in, and when the phone did ring it was only Tiffany, asking if she'd like to come round for another rehearsal session the next day. 'Sorry, I've made other plans,' Michelle told her (well, she *would* have made other plans, as soon as she could get hold of somebody). This didn't go down too well at all.

'See you on Saturday, then,' Tiffany replied coolly. 'I gather we're giving you a lift. We'll be leaving at twelve – don't be late!'

When Yvonne came back in the afternoon,

Michelle told her about the timing for Saturday. It was quite a problem, because her mother had to be at work first thing again that day and Michelle definitely didn't want to spend all morning at Tiffany's house. Mrs Wells fussing around would only make her feel more nervous, and she wanted to hold on to the positive things Ella had said for as long as possible.

Eventually, Yvonne rang Jess's mother, Trish, and asked if Michelle could spend the Saturday morning with them. Trish said of course that would be fine, and she was happy to drop Michelle round at Tiffany's on their way to the swimming pool. So that was that: sorted.

'Can I talk to Jess?' Michelle asked hastily, before her mum could put down the phone. But it turned out that Jess was round at Caz's. And when Michelle rang Caz, the answerphone was on. They must have gone out somewhere. Michelle couldn't help feeling rather left out but, as Yvonne said, a quiet evening would probably do her good.

Michelle had left a message with Trish, asking Jess to ring her about meeting up some time. But there was no word from Jess all that evening or the next morning, or from any of her other friends either. Be like that, then, Michelle told the silent phone and went out for a walk with her mum, who had Friday off. It took a couple of hours for her to swallow her pride and start ringing round again after lunch. She hadn't seen her friends for ages, and she missed them! After all the pressure and tension of the last few days, she felt like mucking around and having a laugh. Eventually she tracked everyone down at Lauren's house. 'Sure, come on over,' Lauren said, so Michelle asked Yvonne to drop her round.

Lauren, Jess, Sunny and Caz were sitting at the big table in Lauren's kitchen, busy being creative. Lauren's mum ran her own business making curtains and cushions, so there were always loads of wonderful ribbons and trims lying around in their house. But before Michelle could see exactly what they were up to, she had an apology to make.

'Sunny, I'm *really* sorry about missing your sleepover,' she began. 'I tried to ring the next morning and explain but you'd already left.'

'It's OK,' Sunny said, biting off the end of some thread. 'Jess told me what happened. You got stuck in London or something.'

'That's right,' Michelle said. 'I was getting a lift with Tiffany's mother and she wanted to take us to this fancy-pants restaurant.' Well, Sunny didn't seem too cross; maybe she'd got away with it. 'Hey, I like this!' Michelle exclaimed, holding up a denim bag that Caz had just finished decorating. 'It looks so cool! However did you make it?'

'You just cut the legs off a pair of old jeans and sew across the bottom,' Lauren explained. 'Mum showed us how to do it: she said all that talk about seventies gear reminded her about these jean bags. Apparently they used to be the hottest thing around.'

Of course, Michelle hadn't brought an old pair of jeans with her so there wasn't much she could do except watch the others sticking and sewing away. But that was OK. 'So what have you all been up to?' she asked, fiddling with a string of purple sequins. 'What's been going on?'

There was a pause. 'Oh, not much,' Caz said. 'Bowling, shopping, hanging around – that kind of thing. How was the audition?'

Michelle told them all about it, and what would be happening on Saturday. But as she talked, she started to sense a strange, awkward atmosphere in the room. The others were being so stiff and polite! They were behaving as though she was someone they didn't know very well, and nobody seemed to want to look her in the face. Jess had hardly said a word, which was very out of character, and Caz was quieter than usual too. Michelle suddenly remembered that she'd never rung her back about meeting up on Tuesday. So that was another apology she had to make. Caz didn't give her a hard time about backing out on the arrangement, although by now Michelle was almost wishing she would. At least that would show she cared.

And then things suddenly got a whole lot

worse. Lauren's mother Valerie came into the room. 'Hi, Michelle!' she said cheerfully. 'We haven't seen you for a while. How are things?' Before Michelle could answer, she went on, 'Isn't it great news about Nikki? I'm sure the others must have told you by now. Lauren hasn't been able to talk about anything else all week.'

'What about Nikki?' Michelle asked, staring at the others in confusion. She noticed that Caz had started blushing and Lauren looked mortified. What on earth was going on?

'Oh, I'm sorry,' Valerie said, clearly embarrassed. 'I thought you knew. Nikki's coming back for a holiday next month. That's wonderful, isn't it?'

'Yes,' Michelle replied faintly. 'I suppose it is.'

She couldn't believe it! They'd known all week that Nikki, her fifth closest friend in the whole world, was going to be visiting, and no one had bothered to tell her! What exactly had she done to deserve that kind of treatment?

'So how long were you going to keep it a secret that Nikki was coming over?' Michelle asked Jess coldly. 'Until she'd gone back to California, or some time before?'

Somehow she'd managed to last out the rest of the afternoon at Lauren's house until Jess's mum arrived to give them both a lift home. But now they were sitting together in the back of the car, she couldn't control her feelings any longer.

'Don't start having a go at me!' Jess said in a low, furious voice. 'You haven't exactly been around much this week, have you?'

'You could have told me over the phone,' Michelle snapped back. 'I rang up last night to see how you were and you didn't even bother to call me back.'

'Look who's talking!' Jess was outraged. 'You were meant to be ringing Caz on Tuesday, weren't you? Remind me what day is it today? Oh yes, of course – Friday. And I bet you weren't ringing up to see how I was. You just wanted to tell me about your latest fantastically successful audition.'

'That's not fair!' Michelle felt her eyes beginning to fill with tears, try as she might to stop them. Why was everyone being so mean to her? She fumbled for a tissue in her pocket. 'I bet if you'd been going to London you'd want to talk about it too. I've really missed seeing everybody these last few days.'

'Then you've got a funny way of showing it,' Jess said – though she was beginning to sound a little less angry. 'What about your wonderful new friend, Tiffany? Won't she listen to you?'

'Tiffany's not my friend,' Michelle replied. 'Not really. She's only someone who's doing the same thing as me. I don't even like her that much.'

They sat in silence while Michelle blew her nose and tried to get herself back together. Then Jess said more calmly, 'Look, we're not trying to be horrible, but it feels as if you're just taking us for granted at the moment. It's like nothing matters to you except this musical – you don't care what anybody else is doing or how they might be feeling. Not really. You can't go on treating people this way and expect them to put up with it for ever!'

'We had a great time on Sunday, though, didn't we?' Michelle asked plaintively. 'I thought we'd sorted everything out.'

'Yes, so did I,' Jess said, staring out of the car window. 'And then Tiffany rings up and you drop us straight away. Friendship's a two-way thing, Miche – not just something to pick up when it suits you.'

'But it hasn't been easy, fitting everything in this week,' Michelle argued. She couldn't accept that Jess was being completely fair. 'I'm shattered in the evenings and I have had to rehearse at home, too. There hasn't been much time left over.'

'Well maybe you should sort out your priorities,' Jess said. She looked Michelle straight in the eye. 'If we were playing Truth or Dare right now and I asked, "Which is more important to you, acting in this musical and becoming a big star or staying friends with us?", what would you say?'

'That's a stupid question!' Michelle protested. 'It doesn't have to be one or the other.'

'All the same, how would you answer?' Jess said, still looking at her intently.

Michelle dropped her eyes. She couldn't lie: Jess would know straight away. 'I'm not sure,' she said miserably. 'I'd need to think about it.'

'Well, that proves it,' Jess said, gazing back out of the window. 'You shouldn't have to.'

Michelle didn't feel like doing anything very much that evening. She and her mum treated themselves to a Chinese takeaway, and then she ran a deep bath, lit some candles, and threw in the bath bomb Mrs Wells had given her the previous Saturday. A lifetime ago! While the water turned pink and fragrant, rose petals swirling all around, she lay there and thought.

She'd been friends with Jess, Sunny, Lauren and Nikki for as long as she could remember, and she was just as close to Caz now. They'd shared so much together, bad times as well as good. What about when she'd had that terrible row with Jess at nursery school and Jess had hit her over the head with a chair and broken it? She still teased her about that sometimes. Or when she'd knocked out one of Lauren's front teeth with a tennis racket while they were playing swing ball in the garden? Just as well it had been a baby tooth. And then there was the time Sunny had won that magazine competition and they were all meant to be going to London to model for a photo shoot – but Michelle's great-aunt had died suddenly and it looked for a while like she wouldn't be able to go. They'd stuck by her then, hadn't they?

But for as long as she could remember, she'd dreamed of standing out there on stage – maybe even seeing her name on a poster outside some theatre. Performing was in her blood, it helped to make her the person she was. Some day she knew it would make her famous, too. A role in this musical could be the way into a whole new world, and she'd probably never be offered a similar chance again. How could she abandon her dreams when they looked like being on the point of coming true?

'Don't forget it's Jess's party tomorrow evening,' her mother called, knocking on the bathroom door and interrupting Michelle's reverie. 'You'd better take her a present. Shall I bring something back from the store? And how about a card?'

'It's OK. I can make one,' Michelle replied, clambering out of the bath and wrapping herself up in a fluffy towel. She'd come to a decision – one which seemed completely obvious to her now.

The next morning, Michelle was up and dressed well before her mother left for work. She'd decided to stay at the flat for a while before going down the road to Jess's – the Shepherds were just upstairs if she needed anything. That would give her time to run through both songs a few more times until she felt absolutely confident about them.

'Good luck, lovie,' her mother said, kissing her goodbye. 'You know how much I wish I was coming with you! Ring and let me know how you get on, and I'll see you this evening before you go off to Jess's.'

'I've been thinking about that, Mum,' Michelle said hastily. 'I might just stay at home tonight instead. I'll probably be really tired.' Well, she could hardly say she wasn't sure if she was still invited to the party.

The next couple of hours dragged slowly by, but Michelle was determined not to arrive at Jess's house too early. At last she judged the timing about right, collected her rucksack and the card she'd made for Jess the night before (she could drop her present over some time later), and set off.

It was Jess who opened the door. 'Oh, hi,' she said guardedly. 'Do you want to come upstairs? We'll be leaving in about ten minutes.'

The others were all waiting in Jess's room, and Michelle felt suddenly shy as she came in. Oh, this was ridiculous! How long had she known them? She was just going to come out with what she had to say and they could take it or leave it.

'Listen, about Nikki coming over—' she began. Immediately, Lauren, Caz and Sunny all started talking at the same time, but she didn't let them finish. 'No, let me get this over with. I was really hurt when I found out yesterday, but it's made me think things over. Well, that and what Jess said afterwards.'

Jess muttered something under her breath that Michelle couldn't quite catch, but she didn't want to stop and think about it. 'Basically, I realized that I've been a complete pain over the last few weeks and I don't know how you've put up with me,' she carried on in a rush, before she could lose her nerve. 'I'm really sorry for being so selfish. Can we pretend it never happened and start over? If I swear on my life never to act like such a drama queen again?'

Caz was the first to come rushing up and give her a hug. 'Oh, you daft pillock!' she said, grinning all over her face. 'Of course we can! We've been feeling so bad about everything too.'

'We wanted to tell you about Nikki, honest we did,' Lauren added, joining the scrum. 'But you were just never around and then by Friday, we'd all got so fed up with you we didn't know how to begin. It was like you'd forgotten we existed!'

'I know, I know,' Michelle said, hugging them in return. 'I'm so sorry! I felt terrible last night when I remembered everything. Missing your sleepover too, Sunny.'

'There'll be plenty more, don't worry,' Sunny smiled. 'As long as you're not too busy going down to London, that is.'

Jess was still hanging back at the edge of the group and, when Sunny said this, Michelle caught her eye. She knew immediately what Jess was thinking. Was she really sorry this time, or was she just trying to get herself out of a fix? What about the question Jess had asked her last night? She took a deep breath and said, 'Look, I don't want to mess you around any more. Maybe I should ring Tiffany and tell her I'm not coming to the audition today. I probably won't get through anyway, and that way I wouldn't have to miss any of your party, Jess.'

'Do you really mean that?' Jess asked, amazed.

Michelle nodded. 'Yeah. If you'd sooner I stayed here, then I will.'

There was her answer. She just couldn't bear to think how awful her life would be if they weren't all friends any more. OK, she might be successful, but there was no way she'd be happy.

Nothing was worth paying such a high price for, not even the lead role in 'Shooting Stars'! Anyway, if she was as talented as everyone seemed to think, there'd be other chances, wouldn't there?

'Well, I've never heard anything so stupid in my whole life!' Jess said, giving her a great big bear hug. 'Of course you must go to this audition! You are a wally sometimes, Miche. Honestly, what a crazy thing to say!'

But she looked pretty pleased that Michelle had said it, all the same.

'Don't worry, you're only about ten minutes late,' Jess's mother said as they pulled up to the electronic gates outside Tiffany's house a little while later. 'It's not the end of the world.' Michelle and the others seemed to have so much catching up to do, they hadn't been able to stop talking upstairs in her room. And by the time Jess's mum had called them three times and they'd eventually got their swimming kit together to come downstairs, it was later than anybody had realized. Still, Jess's mum was quite a snappy driver and they'd managed to make up some time.

'Come on, Tiffany! Open up,' Michelle muttered under her breath as she pressed the buzzer. 'We all know I'm late – you don't have to rub it in.'

Eventually the gates swung open and Michelle dashed through, waving goodbye to everyone in the car. 'It's OK,' she called, 'there's no need for you to come too. I can walk from here.' She was sure Tiffany and her friends wouldn't get on: it would be better for them not to meet.

But Jess's dad had other ideas. He rolled down the passenger window and called back, 'It's all right. We'll just see you safely on your way.' And so Michelle raced up the drive to Tiffany's house with the Fitzgeralds' Space Wagon gliding along behind her.

The au pair Michelle had met briefly on Tuesday was waiting for them on the doorstep. What was her name? Michelle couldn't remember now. And why was she frowning like that?

'Hello! Is everything all right?' she asked, suddenly worried.

'I so sorry,' the girl replied, wringing her hands. 'They go just now! I say maybe to wait some more but they say no time. I ring your house but nobody there.'

'They've left already?' Michelle couldn't quite take it in. 'But I'm not *that* late! What am I supposed to do now?'

'So sorry,' the girl repeated, and she really looked it. 'I don' know.'

Michelle stood there, stunned. She simply couldn't believe that Tiffany and her mother had gone off to London and left her behind. There would still have been plenty of time to get there, even if she'd been much later than she was already, so why hadn't they waited for her? Because Tiffany doesn't care whether you get to the audition or not, said that little voice inside her head. In fact she'd sooner you didn't – less competition for her.

'Is there a problem?' Sunny called out of the back of the car.

Michelle walked slowly back towards them. 'You could say that.'

'OK, so this is the deal,' Jess said. 'We drive to the station. Mum, you and Michelle take the train to London. Dad, you take the rest of us swimming. Then we all meet up this evening for the party.'

'But I'm spoiling everything!' Michelle wailed. She felt so guilty! She knew that Jess would much rather have had both her parents around for the day – her dad usually got totally stressed out on these kinds of trips. And why should Mrs Fitzgerald have to spend her afternoon on the train? 'Maybe I could go on my own?' she suggested.

'No way!' Trish Fitzgerald looked horrified at the very thought. 'How could I ever look your mother in the face if I let that happen?'

'Perhaps I could ring Mum at work and she

could take me, then?' Michelle tried next. But as soon as she spoke the words, she realized this idea was hopeless too. Her mother would never just walk out and let everybody down like that. There seemed to be no alternative to Jess's plan. 'Thanks, everybody,' she said at last, trying to accept it as gracefully as she could. 'I'm really grateful.'

So they drove to the station. Michelle hugged her friends goodbye, and then she and Mrs Fitzgerald dashed through to find out about train times and buy their tickets. Mr Fitzgerald slid into the driver's seat and waited for them to give him the thumbs-up to show all was well.

London Trains - Platform 2

He got the thumbs-down instead.

'One train's just pulled out and it's an hour till the next,' Mrs Fitzgerald told them, climbing back into the car five minutes later. 'And there are engineering works because it's the weekend so we'd have to take a bus for part of the journey. There's no way we'd make it in time.'

Michelle was almost too upset to speak. It was

one thing to miss the audition for the sake of her friends – but to miss it simply because her lift had gone and left without her was too much to bear! If she could lay her hands on Tiffany right now she'd tear out that blonde hair of hers by the roots . . .

'Oh well,' she said, trying to smile. 'Looks like I'll be coming swimming with you lot after all. Let's hope they can lend me a costume at the pool. And at least I won't be late for the party this time.'

'But we can't just give up!' Jess declared. 'We all know how much this audition means to you. It's the final one, too!'

'So what do we do, then?' Michelle asked, trying to keep her voice steady. 'Anyone got any good ideas?'

There was a pause. 'There is one way out of this,' Sunny said. 'I don't know what your parents would think about it, though, Jess – or you, for that matter.'

'I can't believe you're doing this for me,' Michelle said for the twentieth time as they sped down the motorway. 'This is meant to be your birthday treat, Jess! And you'll be spending most of it in the car.'

'Well, we *are* doing it – so shut up,' Jess replied matter-of-factly. 'Anyway, Dad's going to take us to the London Aquarium while you're at the audition. Aren't you, Daddy dearest?'

'If you say so,' Mr Fitzgerald replied gloomily. 'But I don't want any mucking about, understand?'

'Parking's going to be a nightmare,' Mrs Fitzgerald said. 'There may only be time to drop you outside the theatre and come back later, Michelle. Is that all right?'

'Oh, that's fine,' she replied hastily. 'Whatever's easiest for you.'

She was just so touched by the fact that her friends had agreed to give up an afternoon's swimming (and it was a beautiful sunny day) at the pool they'd been wanting to visit ever since it had opened (with a wave machine, a lazy river and four different water slides) in favour of coming down to London so she could get to the audition on time. And the fact that the Fitzgeralds had agreed to drive her there. It certainly showed who her friends were. But of course, she'd known that all along – she'd just forgotten for a while.

An hour and a half later, they pulled up outside the theatre with about two minutes to spare. It was in a narrow road, lined with cars on either side, so Michelle jumped out and Mrs Fitzgerald set off again to find somewhere to park. 'Good luck!' shouted Jess and the others, hanging out of the car windows and waving like crazy. 'You can do it! Knock 'em dead!'

Michelle strode into the theatre, feeling as though there was nothing – but nothing – she couldn't achieve if she set her mind to it. This time, her friends were backing her all the way and she was determined not to let them down.

'You're cutting it fine!' said the man who was organizing the audition, checking off her name on his clipboard. 'Still, you're here now. Come along and join the others.'

He hurried her along a maze of corridors and through a couple of doors to an area backstage where everybody else was waiting while Richard talked to them about the audition. Michelle had the great satisfaction of watching Tiffany's jaw drop when she saw her, and gave a casual little wave that she hoped said, 'Who needs your help anyway? I can manage quite well without it, thank you very much!'

Then, keeping one ear on what Richard 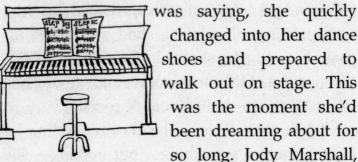 was saying, she quickly changed into her dance shoes and prepared to walk out on stage. This was the moment she'd been dreaming about for so long. Jody Marshall, the famous director herself, would be sitting somewhere out there in those rows of seats, and Michelle was going to show her what she could do!

\* \* \*

A couple of hours later, Michelle walked back to the room where the relatives were waiting, feeling exhausted but elated at the same time. What an amazing experience! There had been another choreographer with Bet this time, and the pair of them had worked everyone until they were ready to drop. But by the end, Michelle felt as though she was dancing better than she ever had in her life.

And she still loved the two numbers from the show – even 'Step by Step', which they must have sung a thousand times over by now. Jody Marshall had come on stage to talk to them about the songs and how she thought they should be delivered. She'd stayed to listen more closely to their voices, leaning against the piano while Mac played. To top the whole thing off, four girls had been asked to sing a verse each on their own – and Michelle had been one of them! Tiffany could frown as much as she liked; there was absolutely nothing she could do about it.

Jess's mother was sitting there in the relatives' room, reading a paper. Michelle felt like hugging her – without Trish Fitzgerald and her brilliant driving, she'd never have made it here in time –

so she did. 'How did it go?' Trish asked, laughing as she disentangled herself.

'It was fantastic!' Michelle replied. 'I really enjoyed myself.'

'Well, that's a good sign,' Trish said. 'And now we just have to wait for the verdict.'

'Thanks for everything.' Michelle leant her head against Trish's shoulder for a second. 'I couldn't bear it if I'd missed this.'

And then suddenly, Jess, Sunny, Caz and Lauren had come bouncing up to join them, followed by a harassed-looking Mr Fitzgerald.

'We finished looking round the aquarium so we begged them to let us in here and they did,' Sunny explained, sitting next to Michelle. 'How did you get on? And where's that Tiffany? Shall we go and give her a hard time for leaving without you?'

'No, I've had it out with her already,' Michelle said hastily. 'She said she'd told me not to be late and they couldn't risk waiting any longer. So I said she wasn't much of a friend if she wasn't prepared to wait ten minutes. Then she said we'd never been friends in the first place. And now we're not speaking to each other. I'm so glad you're here! How was the aquarium?'

'It was great!' Jess replied. 'The corridors are pitch black and Dad hated it because he kept losing us. But when are you going to hear if you've been picked or not? Will they tell you now?'

Michelle nodded. 'They're not going to make us wait till next week. Jody wants to decide this afternoon, so we all know where we stand.'

'That's fair enough, I suppose,' Caz said, settling herself down. 'So now everyone has to keep their fingers crossed for as long as it takes.'

'We don't need to do that,' Lauren told her. 'Michelle's going to get through anyway. She's a star! How could they turn her down?'

'. . . So congratulations to our final nine!' Jody Marshall said, smiling at the successful girls who were all screaming for joy and hugging each other tightly. 'And thanks to every single one of you for coming here today. You were all fantastic! It really has been a tough decision.'

Jess, Caz, Sunny and Lauren all stared at each

other – and then at Michelle, who was sitting there, stunned.

'I don't understand!' Jess burst out. 'There must be some mistake! Why haven't they read out your name, Miche?'

'Because they haven't given me a part, I suppose,' Michelle said blankly, hardly able to believe it herself. Her worst nightmare had come true: she wasn't going to be in the show and Tiffany was. And now, despite her pride, she couldn't hold the tears back any longer.

'Oh, Miche! I'm so sorry,' Lauren said, patting her on the back. 'I was certain you'd get through.'

'They've made such a big mistake!' Caz added fiercely. 'I bet you've got the best voice out of all of that lot.'

'I can't have,' Michelle sobbed. 'Otherwise they'd have chosen me instead of one of the others.'

'You don't know what they're looking for, though,' Sunny consoled her. 'Maybe they wanted a particular style of singing and your voice wasn't quite the right type. Do you think that could be it?'

'I don't know. Maybe,' Michelle said, blowing her nose on a tissue that Lauren had given her. 'Oh, I'm so sorry! I've spoilt your birthday treat, Jess, and dragged everybody down here all for nothing.'

They were in the middle of assuring her that didn't matter in the slightest when a short, curly-haired woman and a tall man came over to where they were sitting. Of course no one except Michelle recognized them as Jody Marshall and Richard.

'Michelle, I wanted to talk to you in particular before you left,' Jody said, and Sunny quickly leapt out of the chair so she could sit down. 'I'm *so* sorry we haven't been able to use you in this show. You sing like an angel! The trouble is, your height and your looks make you seem way too grown-up for any of the parts we have in mind.'

'But we wanted to tell you not to give up,' Richard added. 'There's a future for you in this business, we're both sure of that. So keep trying! I'm going to keep your details and I won't forget about you, I promise.'

'And neither will I,' Jody said, patting Michelle's knee. 'Don't be too said – this is only one setback, you know. You'll make it in the end, I'd bet money on that. Goodbye – and good luck!'

'Thanks,' Michelle said, managing a weak smile.

'They're not talking to anyone else,' Lauren whispered, watching Richard and Jody walk away. 'You were the only one. Oh, Michelle – that's great news, isn't it? They obviously think you're fantastic!'

'Well, it's better than nothing,' Michelle agreed. She felt a tiny warm glow start to burn in place of that awful empty ache of disappointment inside her. And by the time she'd blown her nose twice more, she was ready to go. 'Come on, let's make a move before Tiffany comes over and starts gloating. We've got a party to prepare for!'

Thinking about it, she didn't actually feel that jealous. Tiffany might have got a part in the show, but what else was there in her life? Not much. Michelle had the best friends in the world, so she was the lucky one. Next time she was up for an audition, she'd make certain they were with her every step of the way.

And there *would* be a next time, she was sure about that.

If you enjoyed reading about Michelle and her pop adventures, look out for other books in the Party Girls series. And if you'd like to throw your own seventies party, read on . . .

## SEVENTIES SCENE

Picking a seventies theme for your party gives everybody the chance to dress up in really funky disco gear and dance to some great music. Here are a few ideas for what to wear:

bell-bottomed jeans, platform shoes or boots, satin or cheesecloth (crinkly cotton) shirts, bead chokers, feather boas, glittery sequin tops and scarves, gypsy-style cotton tunics, anything embroidered with flowers, hotpants (short shorts!), fringed jackets.

You can make retro invitations by cutting out bell-bottom shapes from some old jeans (buy them from a charity shop if you don't have an outgrown pair at home) and sticking these mini-jeans on to folded card. Decorate them with glitter glue and scraps of ribbon, then write your party details inside the card. Tell everyone to come in seventies clothes, and it might be a good

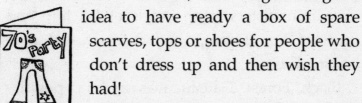 idea to have ready a box of spare scarves, tops or shoes for people who don't dress up and then wish they had!

Make your room look groovy with

some mood lighting: lava lamps give a very seventies feel, and a revolving mirror ball will throw little squares of light across the dance floor (you can hire one from a party shop for the evening). Some nostalgic posters (think 'Saturday Night Fever' and Austin Powers) will also help to set the scene. And don't forget the disco music: the 'Saturday Night Fever' soundtrack, plenty of Abba hits or a seventies compilation album will all be perfect to get everybody dancing.

## Seventies scoff

You can make 'hedgehogs' out of grapefruit cut in half, speared with tasty nibbles on cocktail sticks. Try squares of cheese with a pineapple cube, a grape or a silverskin onion, mini frankfurters (with bowls of ketchup and mustard for dipping), and dates stuffed with cream cheese.

Black Forest Gâteau was a very popular dessert in the seventies: a light chocolate cake with layers of whipped cream and cherries. You can make a Black Forest trifle very easily with a block of ready-made chocolate cake, cherry jam, bottled cherries and double or whipping cream. First of all, cut the cake into slices width-wise and sandwich them together with a layer of cherry jam in the middle. Put the cake sandwiches at the bottom of a large bowl (a glass one, if you have it). Spoon the cherries over the cake with a little of their juice (not too much, or the trifle will be soggy). Then whip the cream with a spoonful of sugar so that it is thick but not too stiff and spread it over the cake and the cherries. Decorate the trifle with grated chocolate or chopped nuts.

## Seventies style

To make a bag from a pair of old jeans, simply turn them inside out, fold in half with both legs together and cut off the legs in a straight line (draw with a ruler and pen first) just below the point where they meet at the crotch. Sew across the bottom of each leg

cut here

backstitch

121

to make a straight line with a sewing machine or by hand, using backstitch (you might want some adult help at this point).

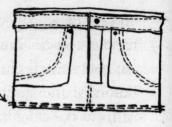

sew here

Turn the bag inside out and sew a strip of Velcro or a couple of poppers at the top (the waistband) to close it. Make a strap out of one of the legs by cutting a strip of denim roughly the length you'd like the strap to be and double the width. Fold this strip in half with the right sides together and sew along the bottom edge and the long side, leaving the top edge free. Then turn this tube inside out (poking the closed end in on itself with a knitting needle or a skewer will help to get you started) and sew each end in place at either side of the bag.

Finally, decorate your bag by sticking or sewing on anything that takes your fancy: fringed trims, ribbon, sequins, studs, fake jewels and patches. The more the better!